2009'

Merry
Christmas
Milo.
xo

Love. Jo & Al
xo

Book design by Kristine Brogno. Typeset in Cochin.
The illustrations in this book were rendered in cut paper.
Manufactured in Hong Kong.

Library of Congress Cataloging-in-Publication Data
Roberts, Michael, 1947 Oct. 2-
Snowman in paradise / by Michael Roberts.
p. cm.
Summary: A magical bluebird sends a snowman to a tropical
paradise for a vacation, asking only that he return to New York
by the next Christmas.
ISBN 0-8118-4264-9
[1. Snowmen—Fiction. 2. Stories in rhyme.] I. Title.
PZ8.3.R538Sn 2004
[E]—dc22
2003017416

Distributed in Canada by Raincoast Books
9050 Shaughnessy Street, Vancouver, British Columbia V6P 6E5

10 9 8 7 6 5 4 3 2 1

Chronicle Books LLC, 85 Second Street, San Francisco, California 94105
www.chroniclekids.com

SNOWMAN
IN PARADISE

MICHAEL ROBERTS

chronicle books san francisco

'Twas the week after Christmas and all through the streets
The snowplows were churning, the ice was in sheets.
And out on the sidewalks, where winds were a' freezin',
Stood mountains of trash bags with old Christmas trees in.

The city was silent, quite ghostly and white.
No parties, no holly, not one festive light.
The townsfolk had left with their friends and relations,
Off to the beach for their winter vacations.

They rushed to the airport with bulging valises
Packed with resortwear that wouldn't show creases.
And no one looked back at the star of our tale,
A frostbitten snowman, exceedingly pale.

He stood on the corner of Hudson and First,
And sighed in the spot where the mud was the worst
"Oh, why can't I travel—do things that I oughta—
Instead of becoming a puddle of water?"

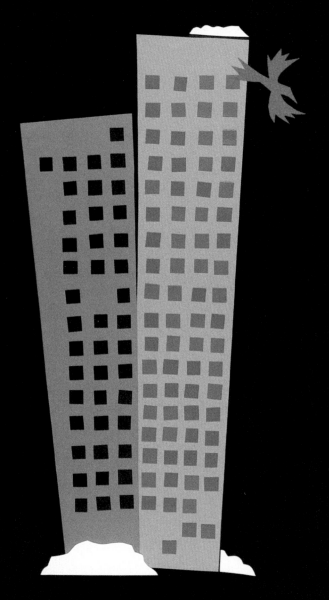

Now, often you wish and what happens? A zero.
But luck was at hand for our quick-frozen hero.
Down from its nest on a rooftop came calling
A magical bluebird, who said, "It's appalling.

"Please cease all this terrible moaning and sorrow.
I'm granting your wish and you're leaving tomorrow.
My magic will see you don't melt in the sun.
Just mind you return for some Christmastime fun."

The following day, though the ice was like glass,
The snowman was off, flying high in first class.
He put on his headphones, looked down at the coast
And dined on smoked salmon with pieces of toast.

He watched a short movie and had a long doze
While dreaming of feeling warm sand on his toes.
"Fasten your seatbelts," a voice then commanded
And all of a sudden the snowman had landed.

The first things he saw were the coconut trees
Swaying on sands near the bluest of seas
As glittering fish swam through bright coral caves
And seahorses pranced on the crests of the waves.

The people who lived on this paradise isle
Looked friendly indeed as they flashed him a smile.
They gave him a hut with a bathroom and bed
And made him a garland to put round his head.

The snowman's routine or his everyday thing
Was to wake, take a shower, have breakfast and sing.
He'd swing through the jungle, find berries to munch
And study the insects right up until lunch.

From winter to spring it was hot as a fire.
In March the thermometer shot even higher.
In April the snowman stayed under the trees
And painted his neighbors, all busy as bees.

In May after splashing with buckets of paint,
He threw down his brush, saying, "Gauguin I ain't."
Then hearing the waves crashing high on the shore
He raced to go surfing and painted no more.

He partied through June, ate bananas in bunches.
He slept until noon and had very late lunches.
Each night he would skip on his big snowy feet
Then pause just because he'd find new things to eat.

July for the snowman was much the best fun:
He'd find things to do—then he wouldn't do one.
He lazed in his hammock, ate meal after meal
And didn't use sunblock—since how could he peel?

Then halfway through August, the snowman said, "Phew,
It can be quite tiring with nothing to do.
Perhaps I'll be good, grow some flowers for friends
To take back as gifts when my holiday ends."

September, October, the snowman worked hard
To make a swell garden that covered his yard.
And then in November he wrapped neighbors' huts
With seasonal blooms mixed with fresh fruit 'n' nuts.

Christmas was coming. He soon had to go
Back to the mud and the slush and the snow.
"How sad," thought the snowman, "to leave this behind."
But then something happened that quite changed his mind.

A sinister bell tinkling far in the east
Signaled the Warriors' Pre-Christmas Feast,
Where hunters who gathered for cocktails at six
Had run out of ice cubes to drop in the mix.

It took just a minute for each thirsty guest
To see that a chunk of the snowman was best
To chill all their drinks, make them taste much more cooling.
"So let's go and get him," the leader said, drooling.

Surrounding the snowman, they said, "You're so cool."
He looked at their glasses and thought, "I'm no fool."
Then off up a hillside he dashed to the top
And dived to escape in a waterfall's drop.

'Twas snowman's good luck that the plants were now friends.
They tied up the tribe, turned them right on their ends.
Then running off fast, he packed up in a trice
And flew back to town where they didn't need ice.

Landing home safe in the cold of Manhattan
The snowman relaxed in the taxi he sat in
Until all the lights shining bright in Times Square
Showed him the bluebird was waiting right there.

"So what Christmas treat did you bring?" it cried, clapping
As inside the snowman's small case it heard tapping.
Then *whoosh!* like a jet out flew flowers fantastic
On stems stretching high to the sky like elastic.

Orchids grew madly as vines started clinging.
Palm leaves and cacti were sprouting and springing.
From Brooklyn across to the United Nations
Each block was a riot of wild decorations.

Shoppers out hunting to buy gifts aplenty
In taxis, which never gave change for a twenty,
Were charmed to discover cab roofs now had gardens
And drivers had manners, said, "Thank you" and "Pardon."

'Twas the night before Christmas and though the snow swirled
Our hero stayed snug in his own rooftop world.
"Snowman," said bluebird, "please live here forever.
This place is my gift for your present so clever."

"To live here forever—how could it be hard?
There's a bluebird of happiness in my backyard!
So here is my wish as I turn out the light,
Merry Christmas to all and to all a good night."